SHARING IS THE NEW COOL

WRITTEN BY JACQUELINE CRANN

ILLUSTRATED BY ABIRA DAS

SHARING IS THE NEW COOL

Library of Congress Control Number : 2022907279

ISBN : 979-8-9856745-0-7

This book is dedicated
to my two boys.

Thank you for the love and joy
you bring to my life.

Love you always!
Mom.

Morgan loved to share. It was natural for him.

It brought him so much joy to see others happy.

Today was the first day of kindergarten. Morgan was very nervous, so his mommy shared a story about how much fun school can be. She smiled and said, "I can't wait until later to hear all about your day."

On the way to school, Morgan and his mommy saw an old man sitting outside a store with a sign that read, "I am hungry. Can you please help?"

They walked toward him. At first Morgan was afraid, but he quickly realized the old man just needed a little help.

I think he is hungry, Mommy. Let's buy him breakfast.

"Not now," said Mom. "We have to get to school."
Even though Mom wanted to help, she was concerned that they would be late for school.

With tears in his eyes, Morgan asked,

"Can I share my lunch, Mommy? Please, please?

"Sure," said Mom. She took an apple out of his lunch box and handed it to the old man. Then she gave him a bottle of water and a one dollar bill from her purse.

"Thank you!" cried the old man.

Morgan was very happy that he did an act of kindness before going to school. "It's going to be a great day!" Morgan said with joy.

Morgan and his mommy arrived at school. And guess who was there to meet them? Daddy! He had just finished his night job and wanted to be there for Morgan's first day of school. Morgan was so excited that he forgot how nervous he was earlier.

He couldn't wait to meet his teachers, Miss Wilson, and Mr. Petti. He waved goodbye to his mommy and daddy and joined his classmates.

Later that morning in math class, Morgan sat next to a boy named Jacob. He was upset because he had lost his pencil. Morgan quickly changed Jacob's frown into a smile by giving him one of his cool red pencils to use during class.

Jacob thanked Morgan, and at
lunchtime they ate lunch together.

Morgan and Jacob sat together during reading class. They both enjoyed reading quietly, and looking at the colorful pictures in each book. Morgan then shared one of his favorite books with another classmate, Olivia. She was very happy!

The last lesson of the day was art class. Morgan loved art. He shared some of his cool art pencils and fun art ideas with the class. He taught his classmates how to draw smiling hearts. His teacher was very impressed with him, and gave him a star for sharing and being kind.

KINDNESS BEGINS WITH ME

The school Principal, Miss Carrington, walked by the classroom and smiled when she saw what was going on.

When Morgan's mommy and daddy came to pick him up from school, Miss Wilson said to them, "It's great that Morgan loves to share. He shared his cool art pencil's while showing his classmates how to draw happy hearts. He is such a great friend." His mommy and daddy were very proud.

On the way home from school, Morgan told his mommy and daddy all about his day and all about the new friends he had made.

They saw the old man from earlier. He waved and thanked Morgan again for sharing his lunch. "No problem, Sir, I love to share!" Morgan replied. Then he whispered to his daddy, "I think sharing is the NEW COOL!"

BE COOL
BE KIND!

Remember, sharing not only makes others feel good, it also makes you feel great when you can make a difference in the life of someone else. Always be kind and treat others the way you would like to be treated.

ACKNOWLEDGEMENTS

Damian for all your hard work,
with the publishing process.

Abira Das for the beautiful illustrations.
Thank you for seeing my vision.
I'm looking forward to working with
you on our future projects.

Richard Crann and Fiona Phillips for always
being available to read drafts and giving advice.

Lisa Collins Bland, Kim Adams, Naomi Dunsen-White
and my sisters in Christ group for
your support and encouragement.

Morgan Holder for your cool art design.

Kimron Carrington and Maliq Royer-Crann
for listening to all my new ideas.
especially the title of the book.
Sharing Is The New Cool!

Printed in Great Britain
by Amazon

86248868R00018